TO:

FROM:

THE
*T*RUE MEANING
OF *C*HRISTMAS

THE
TRUE MEANING
OF CHRISTMAS

SANTA CLAUS
As told to
MITCH FINLEY

A CROSSROAD BOOK
The Crossroad Publishing Company
New York

The Crossroad Publishing Company
16 Penn Plaza, Ste 1550, New York, NY 10001
www.cpcbooks.com
Copyright © 2008 by Mitch Finley

Printed in the United States of America

Library of Congress Cataloging-in-Publication Data
Santa Claus, 1945-
  The true meaning of Christmas / Santa Claus.
     p. cm.
  Rev. ed. of: The truth about Christmas.

  ISBN-13: 978-0-8245-2442-5 (cloth)
  ISBN-10: 0-8245-2442-X (cloth)
  1. Christmas—Meditations. I. Santa Claus, 1945- Truth about
Christmas.

II. Title.

  BV45.S314 2008
  242'.335—dc22

2008028241

1 2 3 4 5 6 7 8 9 10 11 12 14 13 12 11 10 09 08

CONTENTS

One

MAY I INTRODUCE MYSELF?

My name is Santa Claus, and I am as real as you are. Perhaps you know about me. You know that I visit each year on Christmas Eve. I bring presents, both the kind you can buy in stores and the kind you can't find in stores. Oh yes.

Please keep in mind that the most important things in life aren't things at all ... they are things like friendship, and affection, and joy, and the ability to get along peacefully in the

world even when you are not inclined to feel peaceful at all. I bring these gifts, too, especially if you're looking for them. You may ask, "But Santa, where did you come from?"

Listen closely, now.

Listen, and I will tell you.

Many, many hundreds of years ago, not all

that long ago, there was a good and generous man whose name was Nicholas. He lived in a poor country known as Myra, which today is called Turkey. Nicholas was a Christian priest, and he became the bishop of Myra, a country whose people were as poor as church mice. Among his people, Nicholas was known for being kind and generous. Some people today believe that Nicholas was born rich. Some say that after his parents died Nicholas gave away all of his money and riches to the poor. But here is the most famous story about Nicholas.

A poor man had three daughters, the story goes, and the poor man did not know what to do about being so poor. The poor man had no money for dowries for his daughters—which is the very old custom of giving money or property to a young woman's future husband. After Nicholas heard about this, on three nights in a row, he quietly slipped up to a window in the poor man's house. Each of the three nights, Nicholas quietly dropped a small bag of gold through the window so that each of the daughters would be able to get married. Here is another story about Nicholas:

Nicholas loved children dearly, and one time three children became very ill and died. Everyone was sad, very, very sad. Nicholas came to the house where the three dead children lay. Nicholas prayed for the three children, and by the power of God the three children came back to life. The children jumped up and down, and their mother and father were so happy that they jumped up and down, too. This is the reason that children receive gifts on Christmas. Did you know that?

I am Santa Claus, you know, and if there had never been a good Saint Nicholas there would never have been a Santa Claus. Does this mean that I am Saint Nicholas with a different name? Some say yes; some don't know.

I am Santa Claus, and I am the same as Saint Nicholas and different from Saint Nicholas. You decide for yourself who I am. It's a mystery, but a wonderful one. I have other stories, too.

4

In the old times, the people who lived in northern Europe worshiped Thor, the mythical god of thunder. During the long, cold, dark winters the people thought of Thor, and they burned a Yule log, a large log that was burned in the fireplace for twelve days during the Midwinter Festival, and in later centuries during the Christmas season. The people believed that Thor rode on a chariot pulled by two goats, and they named the goats Cracker and Gnasher.

Do you think that I am a modern version of Thor? No. And maybe.

Were it not for Saint Nicholas I would not be and were it not for Thor, I would not be who I am. I am both, and I am neither. I am the same, and I am different. I am Santa Claus, and no one can take my place. I am as true as the heart of a child, and I am as real as the brightest star that shines on Christmas Eve. I am the one and only Santa Claus, and my purpose each Christmas season is to help you celebrate the magic, the wonder, and the love that only Christmas can bring.

In North America I am Santa Claus. But I must tell you that I have other names in other lands. In England they call me Father Christmas, in France I am Père Noël, and in Germany I am Weihnachtsmann. Whatever people in various countries call me, it is always me, one and the same, here to celebrate the true spirit of Christmas in the hearts of grown-ups and children alike. In Sweden they call me Jultomten, where I am something like an elf, and I bring gifts to children on Christmas Eve. In Denmark and Norway they call me Julenissen. I have different names, and I even look different, but I always have the same spirit and the same purpose — to spread the joy and love of the Christmas season. Do you wonder where my name, Santa Claus, came from?

Here is a delightful story. The first Dutch settlers, who came to America a long time ago, were very fond of Saint Nicholas. They even had a picture of Saint Nicholas painted on the front of their ship. In their language, they called him Sinter Nicklaus, and later they shortened this to Sinter Klaus. After these people settled in their new homeland, they still had a great affection for Saint Nicholas, and they told their children that on the eve of the Feast of Saint Nicholas, December 6, the good old bishop would visit their homes and leave gifts.

As the years went by, English settlers in America began to share the Dutch settlers' love for Saint Nicholas so much that they began to celebrate his feast day, too.

Good things have a way of catching on.
But when English-speaking children tried to say
"Sinter Klaus," in their excitement it sounded
like "Santy Claus" or "Santa Claus." As time
passed, my name became Santa Claus for everyone in America. Isn't this a wonderful story? It's
like the little boy who said "scabetti" instead of
"spaghetti," and before long his whole family
said "scabetti" just for the fun of it.

   Is it true what they say about me, that I live
at the North Pole? Yes! But where is the North

Pole? I will tell you. I live at the North Pole, but do not look for me in the snow and ice at the far north of the earth. For I live in the North Pole of your heart, the place in your heart that is the darkest and most difficult place to get to most of the time. But during the Christmas season, with a little help from me, and if you try, that darkest part of your heart will warm up in the spirit of the Christmas season, and then I will return to the world once more, coming from the North Pole that is in everyone's heart.

They also say that I have a workshop where elves work to make toys for girls and boys. Well, Santa Claus has a question for you.

Do you think that the only real things are the things that you can touch, and see, and taste, and smell, and hear? Must television cameras be able to record something and put it on the programs we watch in order for it to be real? Oh, boys and girls. Oh, grown-ups. There are more real things than that!

Do I have a workshop with hard-working elves at the North Pole? Remember, the North Pole where I live is in your heart, and in that same place you will find your love for playing and for creating things. My elves also live in your heart, playing and creating wonderful things, if you give them permission to live there. During the Christmas season, I whisper in the North Pole of your heart, "Give the elves a chance to play and to create wonderful things in your heart."

Many children and grown-ups listen to me, you know. I hope you do, too.

Watch the children and grown-ups who ice skate on the frozen pond in New York City's Central Park and on the countless ponds and ice-skating rinks all over the country. Watch the brightly colored lights and sparkling Christmas decorations. Watch the many, many people who make a delightful adventure out of going to get a Christmas tree. Watch closely and you will see elves around every corner.

Most of the pictures you see of me show me with a big white beard and wearing a bright red suit with white trim, and a red hat with white trim to match. Is this truly what I look like? What an easy question! The answer is yes, plainly and simply yes.

But keep something in mind. The way I am usually pictured first came from a great American writer who lived many years ago, whose name was Washington Irving. He said that Saint Nicholas was a jolly, stout man who wore a hat with a wide brim and baggy pants. Washington Irving said that I ride over the treetops in a wagon and fill children's stockings with presents. My costume changed and became what I wear

now, red with white fur trim, when another writer named Thomas Nast, a wonderful writer who also lived long ago, described it this way. Thomas Nast had the heart of a child. Before Thomas Nast and Washington Irving lived, I was thought to be a tall, thin, elegant gentleman who dressed like a bishop, with a high, two-pointed hat called a "miter" on my head. I rode a wonderful white horse, and oh, I was grand!

But how I look and what I wear is not important. I dress in a special way because I am a special person. I do not dress as you do because I do not live as you live. My whole reason for living is to remind everyone to have hope, and to be kind to one another, and to share what you have with others who have less, and to be glad every day that you are alive.

The reason I am here each Christmas season is to remind you, again, to not be sad and to feel the joy of Christmas. If I dressed in ordinary clothes, that would make my work harder to do. The red suit and the hat with white fur trim that I wear helps everyone to see that I am a special person and, more important, that Christmas is a very, very special day.

You have heard that I travel in a sleigh pulled by reindeer, and you have heard that both reindeer and sleigh fly through the night sky on Christmas Eve. Do you believe that this is true? Of course it is, and it is more fun than you can imagine!

I speed through the starry, silent night skies of Christmas, behind eight flying reindeer, and this is fun beyond telling. Oh, it is very cold on Christmas Eve, especially flying through the sky! But my heart, the heart of Christmas, is very warm, and the love and joy of Christmas warm me from the inside out, right to the tips of my fingers and toes.

It is true what Clement Clarke Moore wrote in his famous poem, "The Night Before Christmas." My nose does get to be as red as a cherry! Oh, every part of my story is true, as true

as Christmas night is long. There is no part of my story that is not true, although much of it is true as the heart judges what is true, not as television programs judge what is true.

There is no place I cannot travel because I come and go in a sleigh pulled by reindeer who fly through the air so fast! What I say is as true as Christmas and as real as the brightest star on Christmas Eve. Do you wonder if I really and truly do stop at each house on Christmas Eve, in the night, after everyone is asleep, and leave brightly wrapped gifts under the Christmas tree?

Some grown-up may say that he or she bought those presents in stores and put them under the Christmas tree. I would say to such a grown-up, What has happened to your heart? Where is the heart of a child you once had? Did

I not say that I live in the North Pole of your heart? Your gift-buying and gift-giving speak to others of your love or respect, but it is I who lead you to buy and to give from a heart that has warmed up some. For I am the spirit and champion of unselfish giving. It is I who bring the gifts, even if you or someone else pays for them.

I am Santa Claus, and, yes, I am married to Mrs. Claus. Sometimes today people want to know Mrs. Claus's first name. You know, we are

rather an old-fashioned couple, and Mrs. Claus is content to be called Mrs. Claus. But if you must know, her name is Emma. Emma Claus. Before we married she was Emma Snoof. Perhaps you can understand why she was happy to change her name to mine! Mrs. Claus thinks it rather rude if people call her by her first name. She prefers to be called Mrs. Claus, so if you ever meet her and want some of her home-baked sugar cookies, remember to not call her Emma. "I am not a woman to be trifled with," Mrs. Claus sometimes says, and you had better believe she means what she says.

Sometimes grown-ups worry about whether they should tell their children about me. These parents mean well, of course, but they need to ask themselves if they have lost their child's heart. I come to add to the wonder, delight, and joy of the Christmas season. Children who believe in me are not hurt by that belief. On the contrary! Children who believe in me often have more joy and wonder all their lives long. They become people who celebrate Christmas all year around. Put yourself in my place. How would you feel if grown-ups told their children that you were not real? Good heavens!

I am Santa Claus, and I am as old as the stars and as young as Christmas. I will always be an old man with a long white beard, and I will always live at the North Pole. I will always make a list of all the children and check it twice. My reindeer will always pull my sleigh through the night skies on Christmas Eve to leave toys and candy for children and for grown-ups who still have the heart of a child. I am Santa Claus, and I am forever. I know this, and I hope you know this, too. Do you have any doubts? Hush.

Listen to your heart. Come closer; let me whisper in your heart. Merry Christmas!

Ho! Ho! Ho!

Two

CLEMENT CLARKE MOORE'S
CHRISTMAS POEM

H ere is one of my fondest Christmas memories.

Long ago, in the 1820s, lived an old friend of mine, a man who understood me as no one has understood me before or since. The man's name was Clement Clarke Moore, and he was a minister, poet, and professor at a seminary in New York City. Clement was a scholar of the Bible, so it makes sense that he would understand the spirit of Christmas. It makes sense that he would understand Santa Claus, too. In fact, Clem never called me Santa Claus, no, not ever at all. He always called me Saint Nicholas. Listen.

In the year of 1822, New York City was like a country town, not a skyscraper in sight. Central Park was like a large pasture. No one had even thought of Saint Patrick's Cathedral, which would be the tallest structure in the city when it was built. Work on building the cathedral would not begin for another thirty years and the cathedral wouldn't be completed for more than fifty years — in 1879.

Here is what happened a few days before Christmas in 1822: Clement Moore sat at his desk, writing, an oil lamp casting its flickering light as his pen scratched away. Clem was writing a poem for his children, a poem he had thought about all day, a poem that would be their most special Christmas present that year.

Filled with the joy of the Christmas season, Clem Moore asked himself about Saint Nicholas, the man from whom I get much of my spirit, and before long Clem's heart told him what to write. He dipped his pen in his ink pot, scratched words on paper, and when he was done he had what would become the most famous poem and story about Saint Nicholas, and

Santa Claus, ever written. He called his poem "An Account of a Visit from St. Nicholas."

That Christmas of 1822, Clement Moore gave his poem to his children; he read it to them for Christmas. When he did, they were delighted. The children laughed, and clapped, and jumped up and down. They asked their father to read the poem over and over, and he did so with tears in his eyes, so great was his own joy, so deep was the joy he saw in his children's eyes. Clement Moore was a happy man. The next year, 1823, a relative of Clement Moore gave a copy of this special poem to a friend, who showed it to the editor of a newspaper. The editor was so impressed that a few days before Christmas he published Clement Moore's poem in his newspaper. But Clem was so modest that his name did not appear with the poem. For quite a long time people did not know that he had written this wonderful poem and story. But I knew. Years later, some people said that the poem was written by a land surveyor named Henry Livingston Jr. Now Henry was a fine fellow, and he wrote some poems, too. But I know that Clement

Moore wrote the poem that came to be known as "The Night Before Christmas." I am Santa Claus, and I know. Because I was there.

Here is Clem Moore's Christmas present to his children, the poem that has come to be called "The Night Before Christmas." Read it slowly; let it rest in your heart. If possible, read it to a grown-up, or if you are a grown-up, then read it aloud with a child on your lap. If you are a grown-up and cannot find a child to put on your lap, then read this good, gentle, happy poem with the heart of a child yourself.

THE NIGHT BEFORE CHRISTMAS
By Clement Clarke Moore

'Twas the night before Christmas, when all through the house,
not a creature was stirring,
not even a mouse.
The stockings were hung
by the chimney with care,
in hopes that St. Nicholas
soon would be there.
The children were nestled
all snug in their beds,
while visions of sugarplums
danced in their heads.
And Mamma in her kerchief,
and I in my cap,
had just settled our brains for a
long winter's nap.
When out on the lawn there
arose such a clatter,
I sprang from my bed to
see what was the matter.

Away to the window I flew
like a flash,
tore open the shutters,
and threw up the sash.
The moon on the breast of the
new-fallen snow
gave the lustre of midday
to objects below,
when, what to my wondering
eyes should appear,
but a miniature sleigh
and eight tiny reindeer,
with a little old driver,
so lively and quick,

I knew in a moment
it must be St. Nick.
More rapid than eagles,
his coursers they came,
and he whistled and shouted
and called them by name:

"Now Dasher! now Dancer!
now, Prancer and Vixen!
On, Comet! on Cupid! on,
Donner and Blitzen!

To the top of the porch!
to the top of the wall!
Now, dash away! dash away!
dash away all!"

As dry leaves that before
the wild hurricane fly,
when they meet with an obsta-
cle, mount to the sky;
so up to the housetop
the coursers they flew,
with the sleigh full of toys,
and St. Nicholas too.
And then, in a twinkling,
I heard on the roof
the prancing and pawing
of each little hoof.
As I drew in my head,
and was turning around,
down the chimney St. Nicholas
came with a bound.

He was dressed all in fur,
from his head to his foot,

and his clothes were all tar-
nished with ashes and soot.
A bundle of toys he had flung
on his back,

and he looked like a peddler
just opening his pack.
His eyes — how they twinkled!
his dimples, how merry!
His cheeks were like roses,
his nose like a cherry!
His droll little mouth was
drawn up like a bow,
and the beard on his chin was
as white as the snow.

The stump of a pipe he held
tight in his teeth,
and the smoke it encircled his
head like a wreath.
He had a broad face and a
little round belly,
that shook when he laughed,
like a bowlful of jelly.
He was chubby and plump,
a right jolly old elf,
and I laughed when I saw him,
in spite of myself;

a wink of his eye and a
twist of his head
soon gave me to know I had
nothing to dread.

He spoke not a word,
but went straight to his work,

and filled all the stockings,
then turned with a jerk,
and laying his finger aside
of his nose,
and giving a nod,
up the chimney he rose.
He sprang to his sleigh,
to his team gave a whistle,
and away they all flew like the
down of a thistle.

But I heard him exclaim, ere
they drove out of sight,
"Happy Christmas to all, and
to all a good night!"

Three

TERESA'S CHRISTMAS EVE

I am a busy man, and even more so on Christmas Eve. My work must be done all in one night. Most people do not need to work on Christmas Eve, of course. Christmas Eve is a time to be home, to be with family and friends, and for many it is a time to join a community of worship. But I am aware that this beautiful ideal is not part of everyone's experience. More good people than you might imagine have a sad Christmas Eve, which you would not want for yourself. I remember one Christmas Eve, not so many years ago. The night sky was cold and clear, the stars as bright as could be. I thought of a woman whose family I had visited many times. Teresa, her name was. Teresa.

She lived near a farming community, her house away off by itself and easy to see as I flew over. I was amazed to see that the house was dark. No cheerful fire, no lively grandchildren finding it difficult to fall asleep on Christmas Eve. Then I realized where Teresa was. I have a sixth sense, you know, an instinct that helps me locate people from one Christmas to the next. Her health failing, Teresa now lived in a place with people who could take care of her. I decided to peek in on Teresa to see what kind of Christmas Eve she was having that year.

The windows of the home were frosty, but I could see Teresa sitting in a large room with many other men and women her age. Teresa did not look happy. She sat in a wheelchair, an old sweater over her shoulders. A television set was on in one corner of the room. Someone had tried to decorate the room for Christmas, but they hadn't done a very good job of it. I was sorry to see that Teresa was not happy. This was not the kind of Christmas Eve she had had so many

other years. I wondered where her grown sons and daughters were, her grandchildren and great-grandchildren.

Why did they not come and take her to one of their homes for Christmas Eve? Did they all live too far away? I wish I could tell you that as I watched, in through the door came a crowd of merry relatives to whisk Teresa away to a jolly Christmas Eve party someplace else. But I cannot tell you that. It was time for me to move on, and as far as I know Teresa spent all of her Christmas right there in that not-so-cheerful place. I hope not, but I wouldn't be surprised. Many, many older people have little joy on Christmas, you know.

I would thank you if you would make some small effort to bring Christmas joy to some older people who no longer live in their own homes. For the more joy you give the more joy you will receive. Think. Think of people who are homeless. Think of people who are hungry. On Christmas Eve remember people who are hungry and have no home, people who are old and lonely. Do something for them, and you will begin to understand the true meaning of Christmas and the true meaning of me, Santa Claus.

Four

DR. SEUSS, THE GRINCH, AND ME

One of my favorite memories of Christmas happened in the middle of May! Sometimes people begin planning for Christmas in advance, and this was one of those times. Just about everyone knows about Dr. Seuss and his famous story, *How the Grinch Stole Christmas!* Dr. Seuss had a wild and wonderful imagination. What a friend of mine he was.

Dr. Seuss's real name was Theodore Geisel, you know—his friends called him Ted—but in his heart he was Dr. Seuss. He dreamed up wonderful characters for all his stories, and this story was no exception. You remember the Grinch, of course, and the Whos who live in Whoville, and the Grinch's dog, Max. Not many people know, however, that I had something to do with the writing of this book.

Dr. Seuss lived in California for many years, and in 1957 he decided to write a Christmas story, but he could not think of a story idea. He thought, and thought, and thought, but he could not come up with an idea for a Christmas story. He wanted to remind people of the deeper meaning of Christmas, but that was all he had to start with.

Dr. Seuss loved Christmas, but he puzzled and puzzled, and no story idea would come. He was very frustrated. Then he realized that what he needed was a story about the deeper meaning of Christmas told in a way simple enough for even grown-ups to understand. Dr. Seuss had no doubt that most children understood Christmas; it was grown-ups he was worried about, plus those children who think that Christmas is about getting lots of presents. Early in the month of May, Dr. Seuss wrote me a letter. He kept it a secret, of course, since no one writes letters to Santa in May. He told no one, not even his wife, Helen, and most certainly not his publisher, Bennett Cerf.

The letter Dr. Seuss wrote to me I still have in my files, and here it is:

May 9, 1957
Dear Santa Claus,
I am having a hard time trying to think of a Christmas story to write. People – sometimes even children – are forgetting the true Christmas spirit. They think Christmas is all about buying things and getting things. I want to write a story so simple that even grown-ups can understand it. Do you have any ideas? I will appreciate any help you can offer.
Your friend,
Ted Geisel (Dr. Seuss)

You can imagine my surprise when I read this letter from the famous Dr. Seuss. Very often the younger elves ask me to read them a story at bedtime, and very often they ask for a Dr. Seuss story. They are fond of *Green Eggs and Ham*, as well as Dr. Seuss's first book, *And to Think That I Saw It on Mulberry Street*. Another of the elves' favorites is *The 500 Hats of Bartholomew Cubbins*. I was surprised and happy when I saw who the letter was from. I was surprised to receive a letter from anybody in May, but I was even more surprised to see that this letter was from the great Dr. Seuss. "Imagine," I thought.

"Dr. Seuss wrote to me, one of his biggest fans, and he wants me to suggest an idea for a Christmas story," I said to the elves. The elves were impressed, I can tell you! I thought and thought for many days. What kind of story could Dr. Seuss write for Christmas? He wanted to write a story that looked like it was for children but was really for grown-ups and children who forget the real meaning of Christmas. This would not be easy to do. I thought and thought. I asked Mrs. Claus to think. I asked the reindeer and the elves to think. So everyone thought.

We thought until our heads started to hurt. So many people think Christmas is presents, and lights, and decorated trees. So many people think that Christmas is a big Christmas dinner. So many people forget that Christmas is, above all, about the spirit of love, sharing, and being kind to one another, a spirit that has no real need for presents, lights, decorated trees, and big Christmas dinners, nice as all those things are, of course.

I began to wonder if Dr. Seuss could write a story that would get this idea across. Perhaps he could think up a mean character who would try to take Christmas away by stealing all the trappings of Christmas, only to learn later that Christmas does not need any of the trappings at all. Here is the letter I wrote back to Dr. Seuss:

May 15, 1957
Dear Ted,

I was most flattered to receive your letter, as I am a big fan of yours, and the younger elves often ask me to read your books aloud at bedtime. I agree that many people, young and old, frequently forget the true meaning of Christmas. I hope you will be able to write a story that will help.

I have thought about it, and the only idea I came up with would go something like this: A mean character – perhaps you could name him "Flinch" or "Grouchpile," or something like that – is so mean-spirited that he despises Christmas with all its joy. All this could happen in Walla

Walla, Washington, which is a funny name for a town, don't you think? You could have Grouchpile, or whatever you name him, live in a cave in the side of a mountain outside of town. He could have a cat named Ratface. Grouchpile could have an old car, drive into town on Christmas Eve, and steal all the Christmas trees in Walla Walla, thinking this would make people so angry they would forget to have Christmas. But in the end, even though Grouchpile took all the Christmas trees, the people in Walla Walla would have Christmas all the same. At first they would get angry, but then they would be reminded of the spirit of Christmas by a little girl – you could name her Mary – and they would get over being angry about the stolen Christmas trees.

I hope this is some help.
Your friend,
Santa Claus

40

As you can see, Dr. Seuss wrote a much better story than the one I thought of, which was not very good. All the same, my letter did get the wheels turning in Dr. Seuss's head, and he wrote a very good Christmas story, loved by countless children, and grown-ups, as well. I always enjoy the fact that Dr. Seuss had the Grinch try to act like he was me. The Grinch wears the silliest Santa Claus costume ever! I love it!

Five

AN OLD LADY
WHO BELIEVED IN SANTA CLAUS

Nothing warms my heart like a grown-up, especially an older person, who truly believes in me. One afternoon many years ago, a man named Joe, who was very good at pretending to be me, was on duty in a big store. Joe was a large man who filled his Santa costume well, and he had a loud, jolly laugh. Everyone said that he made a grand Santa Claus. Joe sat in his special chair and took children on his lap to listen to what gifts they would like to receive for Christmas.

This one day, Joe noticed an old lady who watched him for a long time as he visited with children of all ages. The little old lady stayed around all afternoon, even when daylight began to fade and the shoppers began to go home. The lady watched Joe, a sad, wistful look on her face. Finally, all the children were gone, and Joe prepared to leave for the day. He glanced up, and there stood the little old lady who had been watching him all afternoon. In the lady's eyes Jim saw something, something he rarely saw, even in the eyes of children. Joe saw that this lady truly believed in Santa Claus, and she truly believed that he was Santa Claus—which, in a very real way, he was. He truly made my spirit present!

Joe left his chair and walked over to where the lady stood. As Joe approached the old lady the expression on her face changed from one of sadness to one of happiness. The old lady's face became the face of a child. Drawing near, Joe held out his arms to the old lady. "It's so good to see you!" he exclaimed, his voice filled with delight. The old lady's eyes filled with tears of joy. "Yes, Santa," the old lady replied. "I've been waiting for you all afternoon." Joe gathered the old lady into his arms, the arms of Santa Claus, and gave her a big, warm hug. Joe and the old lady talked for a long time. They talked about the old lady's childhood, about where she had grown up, about her brothers and sisters, and about her grandchildren. Finally, Joe gave the lady another hug, she thanked him for visiting with her, and then she walked happily away, out of the store.

Six

A CHRISTMAS FOR DELLA AND JIM

After Clement Moore's "The Night Before Christmas," my favorite Christmas story was written by a man who went by the name of O. Henry. He lived from 1862 to 1910, and his real name was William Sydney Porter. When he wrote stories he thought it was fun to use the name O. Henry. So that is what everyone calls him to this day.

O. Henry was a great writer, but he didn't make much money from his writing. So he had to take other jobs, and one time one of those other jobs got him into big trouble. He worked for a bank in Austin, Texas, and he wasn't very good at math. He was so bad at adding and subtracting that he made some mistakes, and it looked like he had stolen some money from the bank. O. Henry was so afraid that he made yet another bad choice by running away.

He went all the way to Honduras, a country in South America. O. Henry didn't realize that he would be pardoned because he did

not really steal any money from the bank. In 1896, O. Henry returned to the United States because his wife, who had stayed behind, was very sick. The police caught him and put him in prison for three years.

Even in prison, however, O. Henry

wrote stories using other names. O. Henry wrote a great many stories. In fact, he had about fourteen books of stories published in his lifetime. But his most famous story is called "The Gift of the Magi," and I think it a great story about the real meaning of Christmas. I will tell you the story in my own words. Listen, now. There is so much love and Christmas joy in this story:

It was the mid-1800s in New York City, and a young woman named Della counted her money. One dollar and eighty-seven cents, that was all, and sixty cents was in pennies she had saved by bargaining with the butcher, the grocer, and the man who sold veggies. Della counted her money three times to make sure her count was correct. One dollar and eighty-seven cents, and tomorrow would be Christmas. Della saw that there was nothing to do but throw herself down on the worn little couch and cry. So that is what she did.

After she was done crying, Della dried her tears, took a deep breath, and powdered her cheeks. Then she stood by the apartment window and looked out at a drab gray cat walking along a drab gray fence in a drab gray backyard. Della had only one dollar and eighty-seven cents to buy her beloved husband, Jim, a Christmas present. She must find something fine and wonderful, something worthy of James Dillingham Young. Something worthy of her Jim.

Suddenly, Della turned from the window and stood before the mirror. Quickly, she undid her hair and let it fall down her back to its full length. There were two things the couple had that Della and Jim were very proud of. One was Jim's gold pocket watch, which had belonged to his father and to his grandfather. The other was Della's beautiful hair. If a queen had lived next door, Della's hair would have put to shame Her Majesty's royal jewels. If Solomon of old had been the janitor in the apartment building, with all his wealth piled up in the basement, he would have envied Jim his gold pocket watch.

Her hands shaking, Della put up her beautiful hair. She donned her old brown winter coat and her old brown hat. For just a moment she stopped as a tear rolled down her cheek and onto the worn red carpet. Then Della took a deep breath, opened the door, and was out in the street before she could think again about what she planned to do. Della walked as fast as she could, and when she stopped she stood before a little shop, and in the window there was a sign:

"Madame Sofronie,
Hair Goods Bought and Sold.
All Kinds."

Della ran up the stairs, and still breathing heavily, she asked Madame Sofronie, "Will you buy my hair?" "I do buy hair," the woman said with a nod. "Remove your hat, please, and let me take a look at it." Della undid her hair for the second time that morning, and down it fell, the thickest, most beautiful hair Madame Sofronie had seen in years. "I will give you twenty dollars," Madame Sofronie said.

Now at that time, twenty dollars was a lot of money, so Madame Soforonie's price was more than fair. "That will be fine," Della said. "Please, hurry; take my hair and give me the money." The next two hours flew by in a haze of joy as Della rushed from one store to the next looking for a Christmas present for Jim. At last, she found the perfect gift.

Jim would no longer need to use a worn old leather strap for his gold pocket watch, the one that came from his father and his grandfather. For Christmas this year, Della would give him a platinum watch chain, simple yet elegant in design, a watch chain good enough for Jim's gold pocket watch. Twenty-one dollars was the price, and Della hurried back with what she had left, eighty-seven cents.

Home once again, Della used her curling irons, covering her head with short curls so she looked much like a schoolboy with a twinkle in his eye. Then she waited. Jim would be home before long. When she heard Jim's step on the staircase, she stopped breathing for just a moment. Della was in the habit of saying simple little prayers at odd times about the simple things of everyday life. She whispered, "Dear God, please help Jim to think I am still pretty." The door opened. Jim came in, but instead of his usual smile, he looked cold and serious. He was only twenty-two years old, after all, and he badly needed a new coat and had no gloves.

The second Jim saw Della, his face took on an expression that almost frightened her. He was neither angry nor surprised. He did not seem to disapprove of what he saw, and he was not sad. Della might have expected

any of these reactions. Instead, Jim stared at Della with the strangest look on his face. Della ran into Jim's arms. "Jim, my love, don't be upset with me. I had my hair cut off and sold it because I couldn't bear the thought of Christmas with no gift for you. My hair grows awfully fast, you know, and it will grow out again. You won't mind, will you? Say 'Merry Christmas!' Jim, and let's be happy."

"You cut off your hair?" Jim said with an effort. "Yes. I cut it off and sold it. You'll like me just as much without my long hair, won't you, Jim?" Jim looked around the room, his eyes rather vacant. Then he began to smile and almost laughed out loud. "Your hair is gone?" he asked.

"Please try to understand," Della begged. "It's Christmas Eve! My hair isn't that important, and it will grow back. What matters is that I love you, and nothing can ever change that." Jim seemed to snap out of some kind of trance. He took Della into his arms again and hugged her. Then from the pocket of his thin coat, he took a small package and tossed it on the table. "Don't get me wrong," Jim said. "Cutting your hair off, you will see why you had me confused for a minute there."

Della tore open the package, tossing bits of paper and string every which way. She let out a scream of joy, which quickly changed to crying and tears. It took all Jim could do to calm her down. For there on the table lay the beautiful set of combs that Della had wanted for her own for many months seen in a store window not far away. The combs were beautiful and cost a lot of money, with jewels on the rims, combs to wear in her beautiful hair that now was no more. Even knowing she could never have the combs, Della had yearned for them all the same. Now the combs belonged to her, but the hair they should have adorned was gone.

All the same, Della picked up the combs and hugged them to herself. Through her tears she said, "Oh, Jim, my hair grows fast!" Then Della remembered her present for Jim. "Oh, oh!" she exclaimed. She held out to Jim a package, with her present for him inside. Slowly he opened the small box, and the object inside seemed to glow with something of Della's own loving spirit. "Isn't it dandy, Jim? I looked all over town for it. Now you'll have to check the time a hundred times a day. Give me your watch so I can see how it looks on the new chain."

Instead of doing as he was told, Jim collapsed on the couch, his hands behind his head, a big smile on his face. "Dell," he said, "let's put our Christmas presents away for a while. I sold my watch so I could buy your combs."

I love this story because it carries the true meaning of Christmas. It is the story of a young husband and wife who knew the real meaning of love and the real meaning of Christmas gift-giving. They knew that a gift means little unless it costs more than money. Do you wonder how to give gifts at Christmas? Pay attention to the story of Della and Jim. They each gave up something they loved in order to give something to the other.

If all our Christmas gifts cost us is money, then we don't fully understand the meaning of Christmas. That is the mystery and that is the joy of Christmas.

Seven

A KING NAMED WENCESLAS

One of my favorite Christmas carols is "Good King Wenceslas."

It begins like this:

> Good King Wenceslas looked out
> On the feast of Stephen,
> When the snow lay 'round about,
> Deep and crisp and even.

The song goes on to tell how Wenceslas and his page (a type of servant) faced the "winter's rage" to take food, wine, and firewood to a poor peasant. In the song good King Wenceslas shows that he understands the true meaning of Christmas. The story that the old carol tells may not be a story of an event that actually happened. As is often the case with Christmas stories, however, this carol rings with the true message of Christmas. The song is just a song, but Wenceslas was a real person, who lived long, long ago, and he understood Christmas.

Here is the true story of the real good King Wenceslas: Wenceslas lived in Bohemia, in what is now the Czech Republic, a long time ago, about a thousand years ago, in fact. His father was a duke named Ratislav, and his mother, Drahomira, was the daughter of a tribal chieftain. Wenceslas had a younger brother, whose name was Boleslas. Wenceslas's parents had no interest in goodness and kindness, but he was raised by his pious grandmother, Ludmila. Boleslas, on the other hand, grew up with his parents, and later on it would show.

About the year 920, Wenceslas's father died in a war. His mother, Drahomira, took control of the country. Some bad men gave her bad ideas, however, and she became a mean ruler who was unjust and unkind. This made the good Ludmila sad, so she told her grandson, Wenceslas, that he must take control of the country in order to restore justice and peace. The bad men who gave Drahomira bad advice learned of what Wenceslas and his grandmother were up to, and two of these bad men, thinking that if they got rid of the grandmother then the grandson would run away, went to Ludmila and killed her.

Unfortunately for the bad men, however, a few years later some good men made Drahomira leave the country, and never come back, and they proclaimed Wenceslas the new king. The young ruler announced that he would promote justice and kindness, punish murderers severely, and strive to rule all his subjects with understanding. To prove how caring he would be, Wenceslas called his mother home again. When Wenceslas's wife had a baby boy, about the year 926, Boleslas, the younger brother, was very unhappy. This meant that he was no longer in line to become king, so in true spoilsport fashion, Boleslas joined those who did not like Wenceslas.

Then, on September 20, 926, Wenceslas was on his way to church. In front of the chapel he met his brother, Boleslas, and greeted him kindly. Boleslas responded by hitting Wenceslas very hard on the head, and the two brothers fell to the ground struggling. Some of Boleslas's friends ran up and killed Wenceslas, who said as he fell against the chapel door, "Brother, may God forgive you."

As such things sometimes went in those days, before long the people proclaimed good King Wenceslas a martyr for the Christian faith even though his death had almost nothing to do with religion. Not many years later, Wenceslas was named the patron saint of the Bohemian people, and today he is one of the most popular patron saints of the Czech Republic.

All very interesting, but how did Wenceslas end up in an English Christmas carol? The words of "Good King Wenceslas" were written many years ago by an English man named J. M. Neale. He wrote words to go with a melody from the 1200s. It's as simple as that. Even if the story in the carol did not really happen, it carries the spirit of good King Wenceslas, the spirit of kindness, generosity, and justice, and that is what Christmas is about.

Eight

SANTA CLAUS'S ASSISTANT SANTAS

Every Christmas season, I manage to be in thousands of places at the same time, but that's not much of a mystery. All across the countryside, men — and much less often, women — dress up to look like me. It's quite a tribute, actually. I am so popular that people dress up like me in order to help make the spirit of Santa Claus and the spirit of Christmas present and to remind people of the true meaning of Christmas.

I love it. True, sometimes the Santa Claus costumes people put on don't look very real, but I guess they cannot help that. They mean well, and their hearts are in the right place. Some of my warmest Christmas memories are of assistant Santa Clauses. These people bring so much joy, especially to children and grown-ups with child-like hearts, every Christmas season, that I love them dearly. It is especially thrilling to me when assistant Santas go to visit children who must be in a hospital at Christmastime.

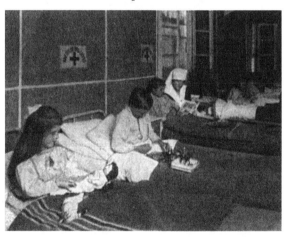

Not too many Christmases ago, I heard about a man named Andrew who was very ill himself. He had put on a Santa costume each Christmas for many years to visit children in hospitals on Christmas Eve, and he did not want to let his last chance to do this go by without putting on that costume one more time. On Christmas Eve, Andrew's wife and grown children helped him into his Santa costume, drove him to the hospital, and helped him get to the children's ward. Until the moment when he saw all of those children — some of them very, very sick — Andrew was so weak himself that he could hardly walk. But when he saw the children's faces he found energy and strength he didn't know he had.

Andrew began to act like me, calling out, "Ho, ho, ho! Merry Christmas!" to all the children. Andrew had tears of love and joy running down his cheeks, and the children wondered why Santa Claus was crying. The little ones who could get out of bed ran up to him and hung on his red pants. Those who could not get out of bed held out their arms to him saying, "Santa! Santa Claus!" Andrew went from bed to bed, from one child to the next, giving out small toys, candy to those allowed to have it, and a big hug to every child. The Christmas joy Andrew brought that Christmas Eve was great, indeed. I, the real Santa Claus, could not have done better myself.

On that Christmas Eve, Andrew was more than an assistant Santa Claus. In a very real way, he became me for those children. When Andrew's family got him home that evening, no one could have been happier. The next day, on Christmas, Andrew passed out of this world into the realm of joy and light, and he left behind a hospital ward full of children who would never forget the Christmas Eve when Santa Claus came to visit with them, each and every one. And do you know what? The very next Christmas Eve, Andrew's oldest son, already a man himself, put on his father's Santa Claus costume and carried on for his father. He went to visit children in the hospital.

Nine

THE DEEPEST MEANING OF CHRISTMAS

I am Santa Claus, and I am here today because of what happened on a dark night under a bright star more than two thousand years ago. I would not be here unless a boy child had been born in a poor little village called Bethlehem all those years ago. The world would be a very different place if that child had not been born, and there would be no Christmas.

I am Santa Claus, and it is my joy and honor to help you celebrate Christmas in your life and in your heart. I help many people celebrate Christmas, those whose hearts tell them that the child born on that night so long ago was

God's own son come into the world as one of us, come to free us, and heal us, and bring God's mercy to a sad and lonely world. Please understand that my message, the message of Santa Claus, is the same as the message of that child born so long ago.

> I stand for love, like him.
> I stand for giving, like him.
> I stand for kindness and forgiveness, like him.
> I stand for light and life, like him.

Like that child, I want all people to live together in peace, everywhere and always.

And I carry the happiness and wonder of Christmas for those whose hearts lead them in other ways. My deep and joyful laughter, and everything about how I look and what I do is to remind everyone of the joy and love at the heart of the Christmas season. I come to remind everyone that Christmas is a time to think more of others than of yourself.

I am Santa Claus, and bringing love into everyone's heart at Christmas is what I do. That is the one and only reason I come on Christmas Eve. An old man with the heart and soul of a child, I come to remind you, children, that you are wonderful. I come to remind you, grown-ups, that you still have the heart of a child. Some grown-ups don't believe me, of course. Some grown-ups allow their hearts to grow cold and empty, and so they think that I am not real. And for these grown-ups it is true that I am not real. But I think that the grown-ups who still believe in Santa Claus and Christmas are better people for that belief.

Ten

SAINT FRANCIS OF ASSISI
AND THE MANGER SCENE

As Santa Claus, my purpose is to bring the true spirit of Christmas to everyone and to remind people of the deepest meaning of Christmas, which is to celebrate the birth of a special boy child in Bethlehem more than two thousand years ago. One of my favorite Christmas memories concerns a man who lived in Italy a very long time ago. His name was Francis Bernadone, and he was a devoted follower of the man that boy child became.

Today most people know Francis Bernadone as Saint Francis of Assisi. People who mainly celebrate Christmas as the birth of the Child of

Bethlehem often place manger scenes in their homes and churches to remind them of that child's birth. Many people do not realize, however, that Saint Francis of Assisi was the first one to do this—more than seven hundred years ago.

About two weeks before Christmas, in the year 1223, Brother Francis wanted to celebrate the birth of "the Babe of Bethlehem"—which is what Francis called him in a special way. Living in the little town of Greccio in Italy at the time,

Francis called for a knight named John who lived there and was a great friend of Francis. When John arrived, Francis greeted him warmly. Francis said that this Christmas he wanted to do something special to remind people of the little child who was born in Bethlehem. He told John that he wanted to build a stable and the rest of the setting in which the child was born to show how poor he had been, how simple and humble he was when he came into the world, how he had lain upon a bed of hay in a manger with an ox and a donkey standing nearby.

John, hearing what Francis wanted and anxious to be of service, hurried off and began to build the manger scene exactly as Francis had asked him to do. It was not difficult to find an ox and a donkey, for such animals were common in towns in those days. John prepared a place where the animals could stand near a manger, which is a feedbox for the animals, and he filled the manger with straw. In later times people would add the figures of Mary, Joseph, and the Child to the scene, as well as the Magi, but this first time there would be only the animals and the manger filled with straw.

On Christmas Eve, all the people from Greccio and the surrounding countryside and all of Francis's followers came to celebrate Christmas at the manger scene. The forest around Greccio was filled with their songs, their music echoed from the very rocks in the land, and the night was lit up with the many bright lights of their burning torches. Brother Francis stood before the manger, and his heart was filled with joy. With a priest presiding, Francis and all the people sang a beautiful Christmas Mass, and Francis, who was a deacon, sang the story of the child's birth as told in the Gospel of Luke.

Then Francis preached to the people about the birth of the poor child, who was also a king, whom he called the Babe of Bethlehem. Francis taught the people how good it is to love little things and simple things. Later, Francis's friend John said that as Francis preached, the child appeared, lying in the manger; Francis tenderly took him in his arms, and the sleeping child awoke.

I do not doubt it for a second. After the celebration was over, the people took straws from the manger as reminders of what they had seen and heard that night, and later they said that when they fed the straw to sick animals the animals got well again. Imagine that.

Eleven

CHRISTMAS IS A SEASON OF MIRACLES

I f the many stories told about Christmas agree on anything it is this: Christmas is a time to expect miracles large and small. I must tell you that over the centuries, I have come to expect miracles on Christmas. In truth, I believe that Christmas itself is a miracle. Yes. Christmas itself is a miracle.

What do I mean by this? I mean that it is a miracle that Christmas should happen at all, that the Christmas spirit should touch as many hearts each year as it does. Each year we hear grumbling about how Christmas has become nothing more than a time to go shopping and spend money. I must admit that there is some truth to this. All the same, even with all the buying and selling, here and there the true Christmas spirit gets through. Imagine. A woman enters a department store. She looks very tired from a long day of shopping. A clerk approaches to help her. The clerk decided this year to work at passing on the true spirit of Christmas. So instead of thinking of the shopper as just another hassle, she looks at the woman as a human being, someone who loves and is loved, someone who has heartaches and joys, someone who, deep down, hungers for the true spirit of Christmas. The clerk says something to the woman about how tired she must be. The woman feels the true spirit of Christmas. It is a small miracle, a Christmas miracle.

It is a miracle that Christmas happens each year. I don't mean to sound grim, but compare the Christmas season to any other time of the year. What goes on the rest of the year? For the most part, people focus on their own concerns and their own worries. Outside of people's own small circles of home, school, or work, and friends, being polite is about as good as it gets. Then along comes Christmas. At the darkest time of the year along comes Christmas, and even the hardest of hearts feels a tug in the other direction, away from being selfish and more toward thinking of others. Even the hardest of hearts opens up a bit more to the possibility of joy.

The spirit of Christmas makes a difference in the world, a difference not felt at any other time of the year, and that is a miracle. Sometimes, of course, additional miracles happen on Christmas, amazing miracles of peace and

forgiveness, for example. Have you ever heard the story of the German and American soldiers who faced one another across a battlefield a long time ago, during World War I?

It was Christmas Eve, and for no reason anyone could think of the German and American soldiers put down their guns, sang Christmas carols, and hugged one another. That was a Christmas miracle.

One of the most amazing Christmas miracles I know of happened in the early 1950s. A man named John was a traveling salesman. It was Christmas Eve, and John was trying to make it home to his family through a snowstorm and bitter cold. He drove slowly along an icy two-lane highway. Suddenly, his car's engine stopped running, and John realized he was out of gas. In his hurry to get home, he had forgotten to buy gasoline in the last town he had passed through. As the car sputtered to a stop, John began to pray, asking God to send him some help. Forty miles away, his wife and two young children were praying, too. John knew that it would take a miracle to get him home that night.

It would take a miracle to keep him from freezing to death, trapped in his car in a storm like that. John prayed and waited, hoping that help

would arrive. After about twenty minutes, suddenly John saw headlights approach from behind his car. He got out and waved his arms. The other car pulled to a stop, and who should get out of the other car but Santa Claus! It was, of course, one of my assistant Santas.

The assistant Santa asked John what the trouble was, and John explained that he was out of gas.

The assistant Santa said that he was on his way to a children's Christmas party in the town where John lived. He would give John a ride home. John locked his car, and then climbed into the other man's car, grateful that it had a good heater. As they drove along, the Assistant

Santa introduced himself as Jake. He said that each Christmas he played Santa Claus for various Christmas celebrations in the area. He also served as the Santa Claus for a couple of big stores, so parents could bring their children to tell Santa what they wanted for Christmas. In about an hour, Jake drove into the town where John lived and delivered him to the front door of his home.

John asked Jake to wait a moment. He didn't tell Jake, but John wanted to go into the house and get Jake a few Christmas cookies and a cup of hot chocolate as a token of his appreciation. While Jake waited in his car, with the motor running, John went into his house, hugged his wife and children, and asked for some Christmas cookies and a cup of hot chocolate to give to the kind assistant Santa who had rescued him from the storm. The cookies wrapped in a paper napkin, the hot chocolate in a paper cup, John stepped back outside … and Jake's car was nowhere to be seen. The snow had stopped falling, the car was gone, and there was no sign a car had ever been there — no tire tracks in the snow, no sound of a car driving away in the distance. Nothing. John stood on his front porch, his mouth open in amazement. His wife came out to ask what was the matter. Where was the man who had given John a ride home? John turned to his wife, smiled, gave her a kiss, and said, "Merry Christmas. Have a cup of hot chocolate." This was a Christmas miracle they would never forget. I can't tell you how many miracles like this one have happened over the years. True stories like this are wonderful examples that Christmas is a season of miracles.

Twelve

CHRISTMAS IS A TIME FOR FAMILY

L isten, now. Here is one of my deepest beliefs about Christmas. I believe with all my heart that Christmas is a time for families to be together. Many families today are scattered far and wide, wide and far, sometimes even to distant parts of the earth. But at Christmastime most people want to be with their family. The airports and train stations and bus depots are packed with people headed home to be with their family for Christmas. People often drive long distances to be home for Christmas. This is good; this is as it should be. People who have no family, or who are too far from their families to be with them, want to be with friends, people they care about and who care about them. For Christmas is a time to be with those we love. I know that sometimes family members hurt one another and become angry with one another even though they love each other. Sometimes family members don't get along as well as they

would like. My goodness, no. In his great novel, written long ago, *The Brothers Karamazov*, a Russian author named Fyodor Dostoyevsky wrote: "Active love is a harsh and fearful thing compared to love in dreams." This means that real life is not always like we hope. We may argue with some family members like cats and dogs; that is just the way it is, but it does not mean that we do not love one another.

Christmas is the best time of all to remember our love for one another. Christmas is the best time of all for family members to say, "I'm sorry," to forgive past hurts, and give one another hugs. For in the long run what do we have that is more important than our family? Friends may come and go, but family remains. Our family may drive us bananas sometimes, but they are still our family in good times and bad. Christmas is the best time of all to remember how important our family is to us. And if for some reason you don't have a family, Christmas is the best time of all to gather with the people you love the most, for they are your family, too.

Thirteen

CHRISTMAS IS A TIME FOR GIVING

Everyone thinks of Christmas as a time for giving gifts, colorful, brightly wrapped packages tied up with ribbons and bows. So important has giving gifts become that people sometimes refer to the weeks before Christmas as the "holiday shopping season." If anyone understands giving, it is me, of course. I'm Santa Claus, and that's my business every Christmas. Sometimes I worry, however, that many people today buy and give brightly wrapped gifts without understanding the true spirit of Christmas giving. For many people, buying and giving has no purpose beyond itself. Which is sad. More and more children think that Christmas is about getting all the latest playthings. What's frightening to me about this, what keeps me awake nights, in spite of all the good intentions all around, is how a strange idea of love becomes a part of what Christmas giving is all about.

Parents and grandparents, for example, often feel that they must buy children the latest playthings so children will feel loved. So children will feel loved! This strikes me as a very strange thing. "If we do not buy the children all these playthings," they say, "the children will think we do not love them." Such people think that they can show love for children, at Christmastime, only by spending money on lots of playthings. They believe they are bad parents and grandparents if they do not give the children huge piles of playthings. So common is this mixed-up way of looking at things that children often believe it themselves. If they do not get the playthings they want for Christmas, they feel unloved! It's a mixed-up situation.

Children, can you help me to remind grown-ups that even when you beg and plead for playthings of all kinds, deep down what you want and need more than anything else is love? Even if a child has a huge pile of playthings he or she will not, merely because of that, feel loved deep down inside. Children, can you help me remind grown-ups about this? Even if parents and grandparents have plenty of money to buy you every one of the latest playthings, you need other things more. Grown-ups need to keep this in mind.

Parents, and grandparents, here is what children need most: First, children need parents who love them. This is the best gift we can give our children. Parents need to understand that buying kids playthings for Christmas cannot make up for them not feeling loved.

Second, children need to learn that giving gifts at Christmastime should express our love for one another. Gifts should not be an attempt to make up for a love that is not there. Sometimes we have enough money to spend on gifts, but if we do not have much money that should not get in the way of showing our love at Christmas. One of the best gifts, for example, is the

gift of time, which is the gift of yourself. Make or buy a Christmas card, for example, and write in the card a promise, a promise to spend a certain amount of time each week with your child in some activity your child will enjoy. This is a Christmas gift no one but a parent, grandparent, or other adult in the child's life can give, and you cannot buy it in any store. (Children, can you remind the grown-ups in your life about this?)

Third, children need to learn to give, not just receive. (Children, can you remind your parents about this?) This can begin when a child is quite young. Ask your child: What would you like to give to your brother or sister? To your friend? There is no need to spend money on such gifts. If your child has money of his or her own to spend, that's fine. If not, ask what your child would like to make—a card, picture, or craft project, for example. Or help your child to write a Christmas letter as a gift.

The important thing is for children to learn that Christmas is a time for giving. We should receive gifts with grace and with joy, of course. But giving is far more important than getting. I am Santa Claus, and I should know.

Fourteen

BAKE SOME CHRISTMAS COOKIES

It is easy to let the holiday shopping season take over. It is easy to let Christmas get lost in all the shopping. It is easy to let the holiday shopping season knock us around, wham, wham, wham. Wham. It is easy to let the holiday shopping season hit us like a wild fly ball. Wham. Of course, when this happens we claim we never saw it coming. Of course, when this happens it is not the true spirit of Christmas that hits us. Wham. It is the empty spirit of the holiday shopping season that hits us, wham. If we seek the true spirit of Christmas, if we want it to come into our life, we must do certain things. We must do certain things to see to it that Christmas, the true spirit of Christmas, can find its way into our life.

We must, for example, bake some Christmas cookies or Christmas fruitcake or pumpkin bread. Sounds simple, I know. But there is something about baking special Christmas foods that fills our home and heart with the true spirit of Christmas. You need not be a prize-winning chef to whip up a batch of Christmas cookies, you know. Children can bake a batch of cookies, easy. You need not have blue ribbons galore from the county fair. All you need is to have a recipe for Christmas cookies and then follow the recipe. All you need to do is make this important, make your desire for the true Christmas spirit important enough to take the time to bake those cookies, or that fruitcake or that pumpkin bread. And before you know it, the true spirit of Christmas will fill your heart like a warm Christmas cookie. Yum, yum.

Fifteen

TAKE A CHRISTMAS WALK

Each year, after I return from my Christmas rounds and hug Mrs. Claus, I love to go for a walk. All my work is done, and I am tired, but there is one more thing I must do before I go to sleep. I must take my Christmas walk. I walk, I look at the early morning stars in the sky, and I open my heart to the true spirit of Christmas. Think about going for a Christmas walk yourself. Christmas Eve is a good time for a Christmas walk. Once your Christmas Eve events are over, take a walk here or there. If you live in a cold and snowy land, put on your coat, and boots, and hat, and take a Christmas walk in the snow and cold. Think about what Christmas means to you. Think about Christmases past. If you live in a warm or tropical land—Hawaii, for example, or southern California—go for a Christmas walk in the warm breezes that make palm trees sway.

Think about the true meaning of Christmas as you walk on Christmas Eve. Or you may prefer to walk on Christmas Day. Either way, go for a Christmas walk with someone you love, and open your heart to the true spirit of Christmas. Away from holiday noise, holiday clatter, get in touch with the quiet, peace, and simple joy that is the true spirit of Christmas.

Sixteen

LISTEN TO CHRISTMAS MUSIC

During the Christmas season, the air is filled with Christmas music. Everywhere you go, in the stores and in the streets, you hear Christmas music of all kinds. Sometimes the Christmas music may seem loud and frantic, which does not add to the true spirit of Christmas. Instead, it creates a feeling of holiday chaos and uproar. Bang, bang, bang? Do not allow that to be your only Christmas music. Make sure to listen to some good Christmas music sometime during the Christmas season.

Whether you are a child or a grown-up, if you can, attend a live performance of Handel's

Messiah; that would be good. Sit there and soak in Handel's music. If you look around, you may find me there, as well. Let the music warm you from the inside out. If you cannot attend a live performance, listen to a good recording.

Would you like to know a secret? One of my all-time favorite recordings of Christmas music is by a group that was popular in the late 1950s and early 1960s, called the Kingston Trio. This album is titled *The Last Month of the Year* and it is, for me, always beautiful, entertaining, and uplifting. Sometimes I listen to it through earphones on my portable music player as I fly through the night skies. If you look, you may find this Kingston Trio collection yourself. Of course, there are many other beautiful recordings of Christmas music.

Remember: Christmas music should not just be background music. Instead, make time to sit down and really listen to the music. Listen, really listen. Let Christmas music fill your heart and help you to feel more deeply the true spirit of Christmas.

Seventeen

CHRISTMAS WORSHIP

I must tell you that after many years of thinking about it, it seems to me that Christmas is far more than just a winter holiday. If Christmas is nothing more than a winter festival, someone who gives it serious thought might ask, "So what?" and "Why bother?" Why bother with all the stress and expense if Christmas is nothing but a winter festival or merely a time to get together with family and friends? An honest person might ask, "Is that all there is?"

On Christmas Eve, or Christmas Day, do as I do, and attend Christmas worship services someplace where you feel welcome. I am Santa

Claus, and my heart comes from Saint Nicholas, so for me Christmas is never Christmas unless I celebrate its religious meaning.

If this sounds strange to you, give it a try. Join the church community you gather with on Sundays during the year. Or, if you don't have such a community, and you are a grown-up, then find one that will welcome you for Christmas, and think about going back there more often. Much Christmas joy waits for you when you connect with the religious meaning of Christmas. Would Santa Claus, who is Saint Nicholas, tell you anything but the truth about this?

Eighteen

BELIEVE IN SANTA CLAUS

Christmas is a season for wonder, a season for comfort and joy, and a reason to seek both. If you are a grown-up you must be on guard. During the Christmas season you must be on guard against hardness of heart, of any kind, against anything that would deprive you of the holiness and magic of the Christmas season. So listen, listen, listen to the sounds of Christmas, especially in the night air on Christmas Eve. Listen to the sounds of Christmas and know that you can believe in me. You can believe in Santa Claus because I am as real as Christmas.

So here is the question: "Is Christmas real for you?" Do you find yourself struggling with hardness of heart when it comes to Christmas? Determine that it shall not be so. Determine to believe in me. Listen. The sleigh and the reindeer are waiting. Come along with me. The sleigh and the reindeer are waiting, and Christmas is ready to be reborn in your heart. Come along with me. The sleigh and the reindeer are waiting.

MERRY CHRISTMAS TO YOU!

Tolbert McCarrol
A WINTER WALK

Few storytellers can capture the sense of the divine as Brother Toby can. In this precious gift book we are invited to stroll along with this outstanding monk through the wintery season of darkness, candlelight, and the rich symbols and celebrations of all faiths. Each reflection enhances our appreciation of its topic, including the Advent Wreath, Bodhi Day, Chanukah, Ramadan, Santa Lucia, and Epiphany.

"My image for this book is a walk in which we visit friends. Some of whom have differing experiences that may enrich us and broaden our horizons. We make this daily walk at a time of year that is often difficult because of the obligations, the frenzy, the triviality that accompany it, and for which our walk can be an antidote. In that emancipated frame of mind and heart, we may find something we hunger for, perhaps the breaking through of a divine spark in our ordinary life."
  — *From the introduction by the author*

978-0-8245-2416-6, cloth

Ann Ball & Damian Hinojosa
HOLY INFANT JESUS

*Stories, Devotions, and Pictures of the Infant Jesus
Around the World*

Catholic storyteller Ann Ball joins Damian Hino-
josa to offer remarkable stories about Jesus' infant
life, including scripture stories and apocryphal nar-
ratives. Photos from around the world highlight un-
forgettable art that depicts young Jesus.

We are familiar with the images of the Child Jesus
in the manger scenes at Christmas, but throughout
the world there is also a strong devotion to the Incarnate Word as a child. From the Middle Ages to
today, the Divine Child has been represented in vi-
sual images, each with its own particular history and
popular religiosity....Childhood contains a promise
of growth. Like the Wise Men who followed a star to
find him, we can grow in love and understanding of
the God Incarnate by meditating and reflecting on
the Holy Child Jesus."
    – *From the introduction by the author*

978-0-8245-2407-4, paperback

Henri J. M. Nouwen
LIFE OF THE BELOVED
Spiritual Living in a Secular World

"One day while walking on Columbus Avenue in
New York City, Fred turned to me and said, 'Why
don't you write something about the spiritual life
for me and my friends?' Fred's question became
more than the intriguing suggestion of a young
New York intellectual. It became the plea that
arose on all sides—wherever I was open to hear it.
And, in the end, it became for me the most perti-
nent and the most urgent of all demands: 'Speak
to us about God.'"
— *From the Prologue*

This personal witness to a God who calls us the
Beloved is the fruit of a long friendship between
journalist-writer Fred Bratman and Henri Nouwen.
Henri is trying to respond to Fred's concern to live
a spiritual life in the midst of a very secular world.
A remarkable aspect of this book is that while Henri
writes to a personal friend, he in fact found a language that speaks clearly and convincingly to all
who search for the Spirit of God in the world. This
work is a ringing affirmation that everyone is loved
by God and can enjoy "the life of the beloved." It
reveals the wonders of the spiritual journey and re-
news the fire of faith.

978-0-8245-1986-5, paperback

Thomas Keating
HEART OF THE WORLD
An Introduction to Contemplative Christianity

Back in print by popular demand, Father Thomas Keating's description of his approach to the practice of prayer is as fresh today as it was when it was published in 1981, one of the first of his many classic works on contemplation

"...the reader's introduction to contemplative Christianity will result in his or her eternal friendship with it."   — THE LIGOURIAN

"This book was originally addressed to those who were not aware that the Christian heritage contains a rich contemplative wisdom literature and practice. Especially written for those who were benefitting from a spiritual practice in one of the other world religions, and yet wanted to retain their basic Christian commitment or to return to it. It was news to many that there was a contemplative practice in their own tradition."
    — *From the foreword by the author*

978-0-8245-2495-1, paperback

Check you local bookstore for availability.
To order directly from the publisher,
visit our website at www.cpcbooks.com

THE CROSSROAD PUBLISHING COMPANY